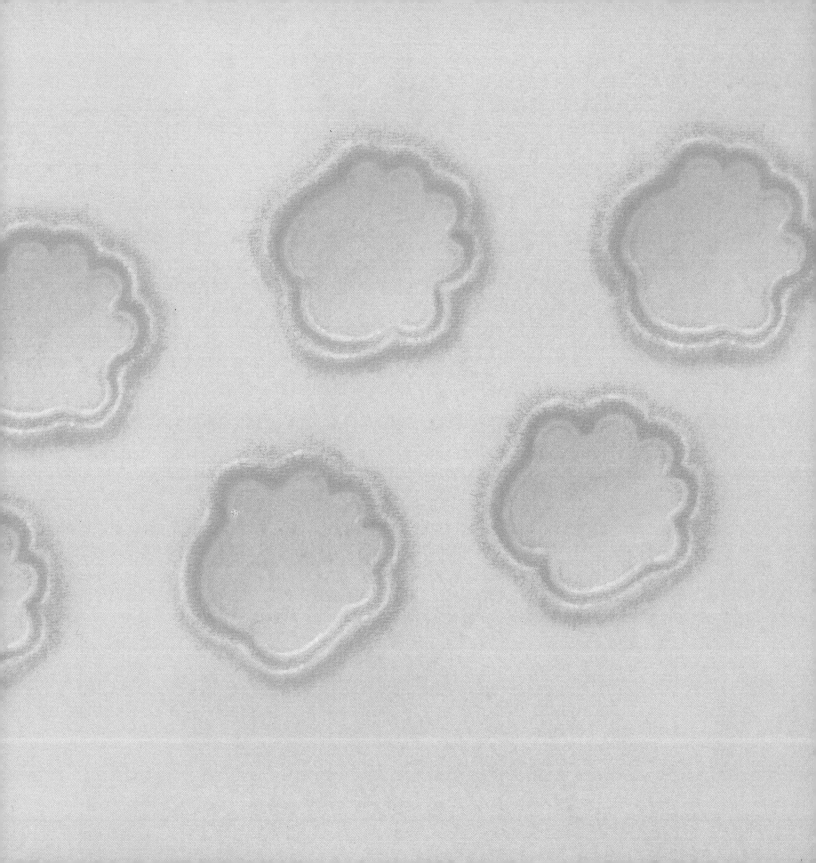

FIONA
and the Easter Egg Hunt

NEW YORK TIMES BESTSELLING ILLUSTRATOR **RICHARD COWDREY**

Z | ZONDER**kidz**

To my friends at Paragraph's Bookstore.
—RC

ZONDERKIDZ

Fiona and the Easter Egg Hunt
Copyright © 2024 by Zondervan
Illustrations © 2024 by Zondervan

Requests for information
should be addressed to:
Zonderkidz, Grand Rapids, Michigan 49546

Hardcover: 978-0-310-14399-4
Ebook: 978-0-310-14400-7
Audio Download: 978-0-310-14401-4

Library of Congress Cataloging-in-Publication Data

Names: Cowdrey, Richard, illustrator.
Title: Fiona and the Easter egg hunt / illustrated by Richard Cowdrey.
Description: Grand Rapids, Michigan : Zonderkidz, [2023] | Series: A Fiona
the hippo book | Audience: Ages 4-8. | Summary: Fiona plans an Easter
egg hunt for all her friends at the zoo.
Identifiers: LCCN 2022034892 (print) | LCCN 2022034893 (ebook) | ISBN
9780310143994 (hardcover) | ISBN 9780310144007 (ebook)
Subjects: CYAC: Easter egg hunts--Fiction. | Fiona (Hippopotamus),
2017---Fiction. | Hippopotamus--Fiction. | Zoo animals--Fiction. |
LCGFT: Animal fiction. | Picture books.
Classification: LCC PZ7.1.C685 Fbm 2023 (print) | LCC PZ7.1.C685 (ebook)
| DDC [E]--dc23
LC record available at https://lccn.loc.gov/2022034892
LC ebook record available at https://lccn.loc.gov/2022034893

Any internet addresses (websites, blogs, etc.) and telephone numbers in this book are offered as
a resource. They are not intended in any way to be or imply an endorsement by Zondervan, nor does
Zondervan vouch for the content of these sites and numbers for the life of this book.

Illustrated by: Richard Cowdrey
Contributors: Barbara Herndon and Mary Hassinger
Art direction and design: Cindy Davis

Printed in Malaysia

24 25 26 27 28 /COS/ 20 19 18 17 16 15 14 13 12 11 10 9 8 7 6 5 4 3 2 1

It was a beautiful spring day. Everywhere Fiona looked there were new and colorful things ... the sunshine was just a little warmer ... the grass was just a little greener ... and flowers were popping up all over the zoo.

And something else was popping up too ...

BABIES! Lots and lots of babies were being born, saying hello to their mamas and daddies and visitors at the zoo. It was an exciting time.

As Fiona and her friend Rico the porcupine wandered around greeting their new little friends, Rico saw a big, bright sign that said, "Easter Egg Hunt Coming SOON!"

"What's an Easter egg hunt, Fiona?"

"It's when someone hides a bunch of eggs with treats inside and people have fun finding them," Fiona explained.

"Oooh, I want to do that!" Rico squealed.

Fiona had a wonderful idea.
"Why don't WE have an Easter egg hunt for all our animal friends?"

Fiona and Rico got busy making colorful
paper-mache eggs and filling them with treats.
They even made lovely invitations for the big event.

Finally, Fiona the Easter Hippo was ready! She and Rico couldn't wait to hide their beautiful eggs around the zoo.

"This is so much fun!" Fiona whispered. She tucked an egg in the reeds near the duck pond, and Rico climbed up to put one on a leafy tree branch.

As Fiona watched Rico hide the egg, Mrs. Swan came waddling by. "Hello, Fiona. What are you and Rico up to?"

"Oh, nothing … " said Fiona, trying to keep her hiding places a secret. "Have your babies hatched, Mrs. Swan?" Fiona knew six swan babies were coming soon.

"No, not yet. I'm going to look for some bits of grass and leaves to make my nest cozier for their arrival. Fiona, could you and Rico watch my eggs while I'm gone?"

"Of course!" said Fiona. Then she wiggled her ears, let out a snort, and said, "We've got this!"

Fiona looked at the swan eggs in awe. She thought she'd snuggle up next to them, just like Mama snuggled her when she was sleepy. But Fiona was a growing hippo. As she wiggled closer, she bumped right into the nest and the basket of Easter eggs.

Eggs rolled everywhere!

"I'll get them," said Rico, as Fiona carefully nudged swan eggs back in the nest.

"Thanks," said Fiona, laying back down to keep the babies warm.

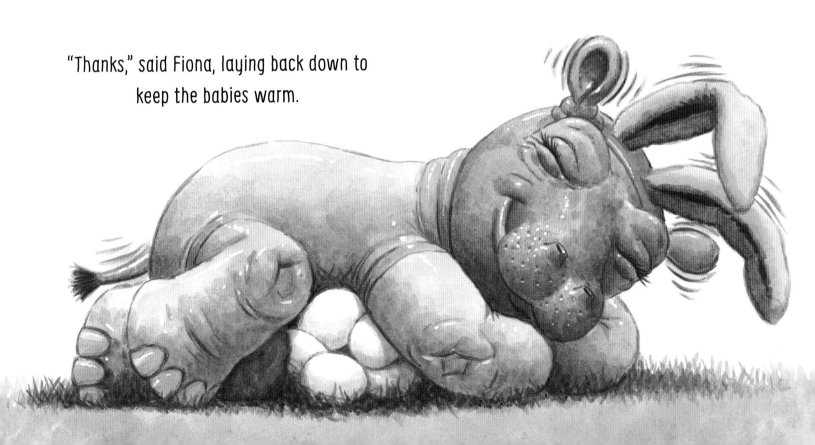

Fiona and Rico took their egg-sitting job seriously.

They snuggled the swan eggs, they read them a good book, they sang a song, and they even told the eggs about the Easter egg hunt planned for later that day.

When Mrs. Swan returned, she thanked her friends.
"You are such great helpers!" she said as she tucked
sweet-smelling grass and fresh green leaves around
the nest and sat back down on her eggs.

Fiona and Rico waved goodbye
and set out to finish hiding the
rest of the Easter eggs.

They tucked eggs into bushes.

They slid eggs under leaves.

They floated eggs on lily pads.

And Rico climbed lots of trees, looking for just the right hiding spots for their taller friends like Giraffe and Elephant.

When the very last egg was hidden, Fiona and Rico were ready to start the hunt!

As Fiona the Easter Hippo welcomed
everyone to the big event,
GRUNTS and SQUAWKS and ROARS
of excitement rang through the zoo.

Suddenly, above all the other noises,
came a loud trumpeting call!

"Oh-OH!! Oh-OH!! My egg is MISSING!"
cried Mrs. Swan, her big wings flapping an alarm.

Mrs. Swan's call was the loudest sound Fiona had ever heard! Mama and Fiona ran off to the pond with the other animals to see what was wrong.

"What's the matter?" asked Fiona. "Can we help?"

"One of my eggs is missing!

I had six and now there are only five!!! It is small
and creamy white, and it's almost ready to hatch!
Please, help me find my egg!!!"

Rico's eyes grew wide. Then he leaned close and whispered in
Fiona's ear, "Fiona, remember when the Easter basket tipped over?
Could we have put the egg in our basket?"

"I don't know," Fiona replied.

"If that's what happened, we need to find that egg," Mama said.

"Don't worry, we'll find it!" said Fiona. "We've got this!"

Fiona called to all her friends. "Gather round, everyone! We're going to go on an EXTRA SPECIAL Easter Egg Hunt! We hid eggs all over the zoo for you to find. They are all colorful except one—one is pretty and white and very special to Mrs. Swan. It's her missing egg. Now, let the hunt begin!"

The animals ran off in every direction.

They found purple and pink and
blue eggs in the trees.

They found yellow
and orange and green
eggs in the bushes
and tall grass.

They even found striped and polka-dotted eggs!

But no one found a small white egg.

Just when it seemed like the animals had looked everywhere, Fiona remembered something ...
Rico had tucked some eggs under a patch of pretty pink flowers. Had anyone looked there?

Fiona nuzzled her way into the flowerbed. But she did not see an egg.

"WAIT! What's that?" Rico squealed, pointing at a tiny white spot in the grass.
"And that? And that too?"

As Fiona and Rico followed the trail of white bits and pieces, they heard something ... a little squeaky PEEP. And a CRACK. And there, waddling across the grass, was the missing egg!

"Look! That egg has LEGS!" shouted Fiona.

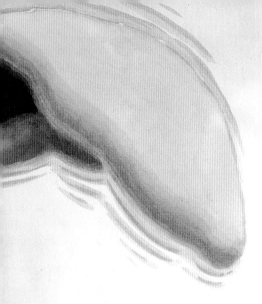

Fiona lowered her nose closer to the little egg and something wonderful happened.
The rest of the egg cracked away. It was the most beautiful baby swan Fiona had ever seen.

"Mama?" peeped the little swan as he waddled up to Fiona's big hippo nose for a nuzzle.

"Welcome to the world, little one!"

The animals at the zoo had many things to celebrate that spring day!

The missing baby swan had been found safe and sound.

It was a special day called Easter.

Fiona and Rico had treated their friends to the first ever Animal Friends Easter Egg Hunt.

And there were lots and lots of babies to welcome to the zoo.

But even though it was a great day, there was still one itty-bitty problem ...

No matter what Fiona did,
the little swan followed her EVERYWHERE!

But Fiona didn't really mind.
She loved the fluffy little fellow.

That night, a tired Fiona cuddled up to sleep, the baby swan nuzzled under her chunky chin.

"I'm glad Mama let us have a sleepover," whispered Fiona.

"Hush now, Fiona," called Mama from nearby. "Get some sleep."

And they did.

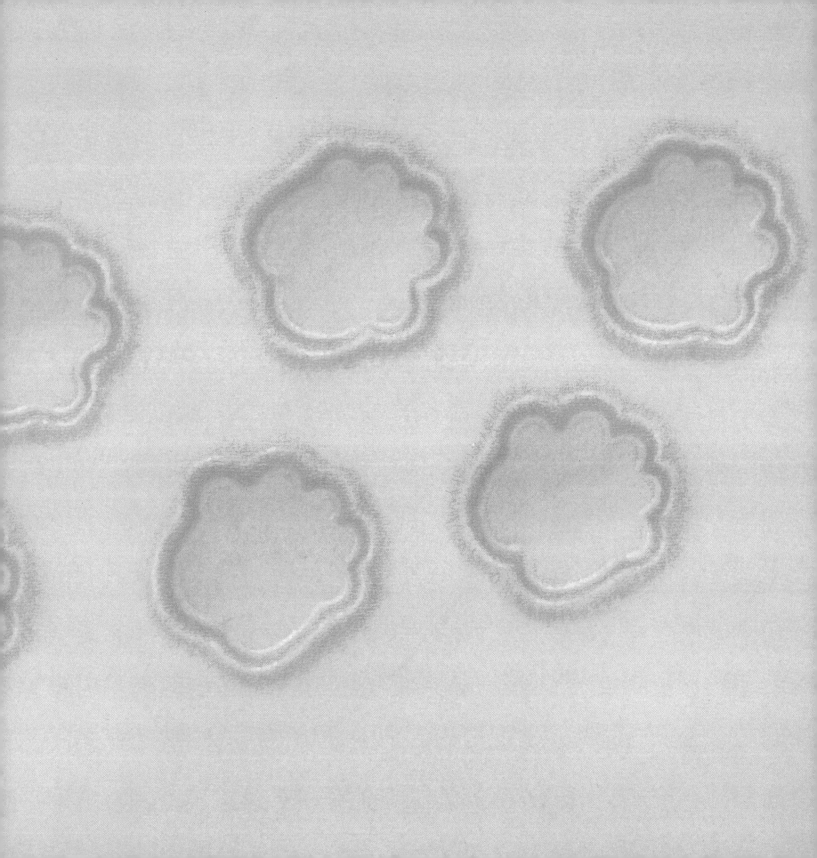

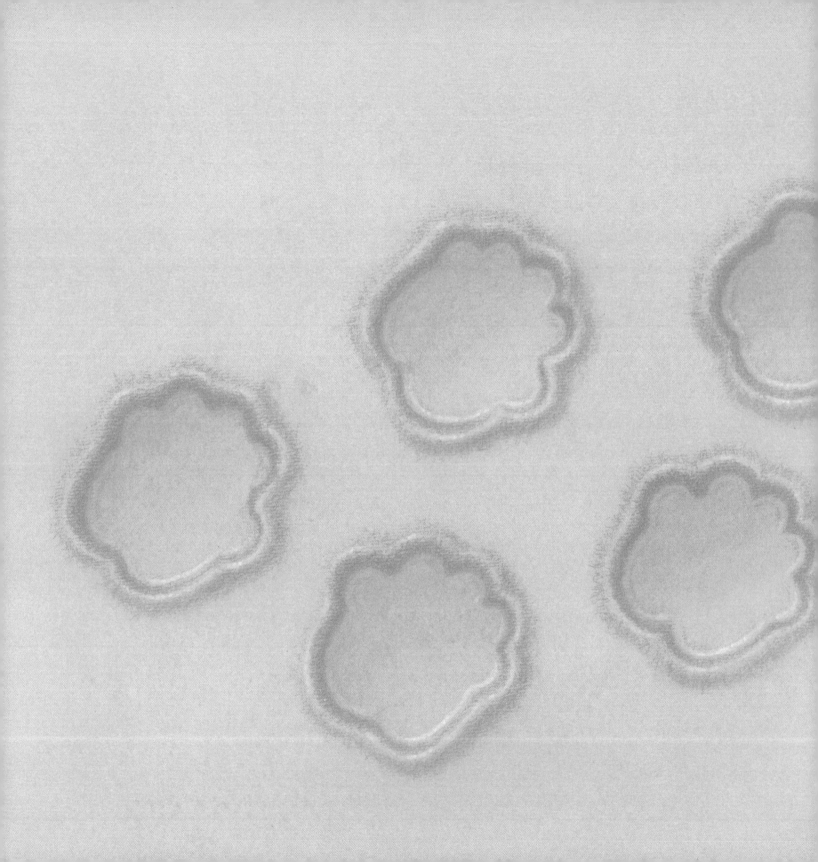